I0626301

Valentine's Day at Glosser's

By Robert Jeschonek

pie press publishing

pie press publishing
www.piepresspublishing.com

The text was set in Myriad Pro and Garamond.
Book design by Robert Jeschonek
ISBN-10: 0998576107
ISBN-13: 9780998576107

Love is in the air at Gee Bee and Glosser Bros.

"Do you think we'll ever find the unknown poet?" asked Emily.

"I honestly don't know," said Ryan.

"But we *have* to. We can't give up!"

"I knew you'd say that." Ryan smiled.

"Really?" Emily laughed. "But we've only known each other a few days."

"Sometimes that's all it takes." Ryan met her gaze. "Sometimes, you just *know* somebody from the start."

Emily looked away. What was it about him that made her blush sometimes?

"It's been fun, hasn't it?" said Ryan. "Working together, solving the mystery. Just like when two people are solving a crime in a movie. They investigate and find clues, and the mystery deepens." He stopped in front of the Central Park gazebo and turned to face her. "Then they have a moment where he takes her hand." He reached for her hand, and she didn't pull it away. "Then the music swells, and he tells her how he really feels."

Emily's heart pounded. She was caught up in the magic of the moment, the feel of his hand, the sparkle in his eyes...the wondering what would come next.

Ryan leaned closer. The mist of his breath mingled with hers as he spoke.

"Then he tells her he's come to care for her, and he can't stop thinking about her, and he can't bear to be without her." He smiled.

Emily thought he might kiss her...

DEDICATION

To the men and women of Gee Bee, who
made us fall in love with their wonderful
store again and again.

The contents of the mail sack poured onto a round table in the break room of the Gee Bee Department Store—hundreds of postcards and letters addressed to a woman who didn't exist.

Though the woman sitting at the table was known to answer to her name.

"Just look at all those cards and letters," said Gary the mailroom guy. "Every one of them made out to you, Miss Gee Bee."

"What can I say? My fans adore me." The smiling woman at the table was young and pretty, with deep green eyes and shoulder-length black hair. "I guess 1973 is the year I hit it big." Though she wasn't really named "Miss Gee Bee," she played that character in ads for the Gee Bee discount department stores, offshoots of the legendary Glosser Bros. store in Johnstown, Pennsylvania.

Her *real* name was Emily Bradley.

"Well, enjoy the adoration." Gary shook out a few last cards and slung the empty bag over his shoulder. "Looks like you've got a couple *hours'* worth to keep you busy, Miss Gee Bee."

"Feel free to jump in and give me a hand." Emily scooped up a stack of cards and letters and shook them emphatically. "Come on, Gary! Don't tell me you don't love romantic *poetry*."

"Okay, I won't tell you." Gary chuckled as he headed for the door. "But I *might* have been known to *write* some from time to time."

"Oh my God! You mean..." She scooped up some mail and gazed at it wonderingly. "One of *these* could be *your entry* for the big *contest?*"

"You never know, Miss Gee Bee." Gary grinned and spoke along the back of his hand as if telling her a secret. "P.S., I *might* have signed it with a *pen name*."

"Then how will I know it's yours?" asked Emily.

"You'll know when it makes you swoon," said Gary.

"*Throw up* is more like it," said Emily's friend and co-worker, Tina Fontana, as she strolled past Gary into the room. "Save it for the girls at the warehouse, Gare."

"I've got a poem for you, too, Tina," said Gary. "It starts with 'There once was a girl from Nantucket.'"

"Always so charming, Gare." Tina rolled her eyes and gave her long blonde hair a toss.

"Then why did you go out with me that time?"

"Beats the heck outta me." Tina spun to smile at

Emily as Gary slunk out of the room, mumbling. "So check *you* out, honey. You're really raking in the *valentines.*"

"Don't be jealous," said Emily. "They're for Miss Gee Bee."

"You must feel so *special.*" Tina picked up a postcard, read the message on the back, and fanned herself with it. "All these romantic *poems.*"

"Which aren't even all from *guys.*"

"They aren't?"

"I can tell." Emily nodded emphatically. "The really *good* ones are from *women.*"

"I'll bet they said that to Bill Shakespeare."

"Shakespeare didn't write love poems to win a 10% Sweetheart Shopping Spree at Gee Bee Department Store." Emily picked up a handful of mail and let it dribble down onto the pile. "Trust me, there's no Shakespeare in *this* mess."

"Whose idea *was* this contest anyway?" Tina scowled as she read another card, then threw it right in a nearby trash can. "Jack Shepherd?" She was talking about the manager of the store.

"Straight from the top, I heard." Emily rolled her eyes. "Mr. Black himself."

Tina chuckled. "You really *are* on the radar, girl! Better mind your P's and Q's."

Just then, Gary leaned in the doorway and whistled. When Emily and Tina looked, he threw a paper airplane, which floated in their direction...and suddenly crashed.

"Geez," said Tina. "You can't even make a *paper plane* right."

"Just what we needed, Gary." Emily didn't bother picking up the plane. "More *poetry.*"

"Not poetry." Gary smirked. "A message from the *boss.*"

"But Mr. Shepherd could've just walked back here and told her himself," said Tina. "Why the paperwork?"

"I'm talking about the *big* boss." Gary nodded as he backed out the door. "The boss in downtown *Johnstown.*"

Tina bugged her eyes wide. "Speak of the devil!"

Emily jumped up and grabbed the plane from the floor. Before she unfolded it and read the note inside, she already knew who'd written it. She knew exactly whom Gary was talking about.

Gee Bee was a suburban store in Richland Township. The mother store, Glosser Bros., was located a few miles away in downtown Johnstown. That was where the biggest bigwigs could be found, including the company president.

Getting called to see him, Emily knew, could be a big deal—for better or worse.

"Have fun, Miss Gee Bee!" said Gary as he slipped back out of the break room.

"Go Gee Bee yourself, Gare!" Tina told him.

Emily folded the note and stuck it in the pocket of her black slacks. "I guess I'd better get going. The note says I need to see the president right away."

"About what?" asked Tina.

"It doesn't say." A feeling of dread crept over Emily. She couldn't think of anything she might have done wrong—but she still worried about the summons. Her profile had been raised three months ago, when the bosses had chosen her as the real-life version of company mascot Miss Gee Bee; ever since, as a company representative, she'd had to stay on her best behavior and had been more worried about getting in trouble.

It wasn't easy being Miss Gee Bee.

"Maybe he just wants to give you a love poem, too," said Tina.

"Good." Emily straightened her floral print button-down blouse, checked her hair in the mirror, and grabbed her purse from the back of the chair where she'd been sitting. "It has to be better than anything *Gary* comes up with."

*****

When Emily walked in the front door of the Glosser Bros. Department Store in downtown Johnstown, the first thing that struck her, as always, was the wonderful smell of roasting peanuts and cashews. It was a smell that always made her feel at home, a smell that had been part of her life for as long as she remembered. It made her feel welcome, whether she entered as an employee or shopper.

And it drew her onward, through the first floor of the store, which was busy even then, at lunchtime on a

Wednesday in early February. The source of the roasted nut fragrance—the candy and nut counter—came up shortly after she entered, and she wished she had time to stop for a snack.

Further along, women in winter coats browsed the bargain tables on the Locust Street side of the floor, sifting through gloves, handbags, hats, and more. Across from the women's accessories, old men and a few middle-aged businessmen on lunch break wandered through the men's furnishings area, picking through socks, t-shirts, underwear, and ties.

Emily waved at sales people she knew but didn't stop to chat; she couldn't, with the president waiting for her. A good friend who worked for a downtown bank was coming down the escalator from the second floor, but Emily ducked her head and kept going, avoiding an encounter.

Finally, she made it to the elevator bank along the side of the store facing Locust Street and Central Park. She punched the button for the upper floors, and a car arrived a moment later. After a woman with two small children got off, Emily boarded the car and hit the button for the fourth floor, where the corporate management offices were located.

The elevator dinged, the door slid open, and she stepped out onto the fourth floor. Passing the home furnishings and housewares departments, she reached her destination—the office of the president of the company, who had summoned her from Gee Bee in Richland.

Opening the door, she saw the secretary in the outer office was away from her desk...but the inner office wasn't empty at all.

"Hello? Who's there?"

"Emily Bradley." Nervous, she peeked around the corner of the inner office.

President Leonard Black smiled back at her from behind his big desk. "Come in, come in." He patted his silver hair and got to his feet. "Thank you for stopping down, Miss Bradley."

"Thank you, sir." Emily stepped inside, her heart pounding as she wondered about the object of the meeting.

It was only then that she saw someone else was in the room, standing just inside the doorway. It was a young man she didn't recognize, with curly black hair and a wide, dimpled grin. She could see, from the way his navy blue leisure suit hung from his body, that he was athletic, with broad, muscular shoulders, beefy arms, and a lean, tapered midriff.

"Emily Bradley—Miss Gee Bee—I'd like you to meet Ryan Morgan." President Black gestured at the dark-haired man and smiled. "Otherwise known as Glossy the Glosser Boy."

"Nice to meet you, Emily." Ryan nodded and reached for a handshake.

Emily returned it, though she was confused. "Glossy the Glosser Boy?" She'd never heard the name before.

"Our brand-new mascot." President Black nodded.

"Like Miss Gee Bee for the Glosser Bros. store."

"Right." Emily almost always made it a point to agree with the boss. "Nice to meet you, Ryan."

"We're phasing in the character." President Black held up a sheet of paper with "Glossy the Glosser Boy" printed alongside a drawing of a young man's smiling face—identical to Miss Gee Bee except for the shorter hair. "Eventually, he'll be in ads, on shopping bags, on billboards, just like you."

"That's neat," said Emily, though she didn't really think it was neat.

"And we'll start with the two of you together," said President Black. "Judging the Valentine's contest."

"Okay." Emily was becoming less thrilled by the minute.

"We've started telling people they can send poems to one or the other of you," explained President Black. "If the winning entry is written for you, Emily, the Sweetheart Shopping Spree will happen at Gee Bee in Richland. But if Ryan gets the winner, the spree will happen right here at Glosser Bros."

"Nothing like a little friendly competition." Ryan smiled. "Am I right, Emily?"

"So, wait." Emily frowned. "The *two* of us are supposed to judge the contest entries *together?*"

"Correct." President Black walked over to stand between them, putting his hands on their shoulders. "And to keep it fair, I want you to work here at Glosser's one day and up at Gee Bee the next. How does that strike you?"

"Just fine," said Emily, though it didn't strike her well at all. She worked at Gee Bee in Richland and lived just a few miles away in Geistown; running to downtown Johnstown every other day would be a pain.

"What a great idea," said Ryan. "Miss Gee Bee and Glossy the Glosser Boy, working together! People should really get a kick out of it."

"Can't hurt to give it a try," said President Black. "The folks in marketing think it has legs, so we'll see."

"I'll keep my fingers crossed," said Emily, though she didn't mean it.

"Now get downstairs on the sales floor, you two," said President Black. "I want you to judge the contest so everyone can see you. That'll really get 'em in the mood."

"Yes, sir," said Emily.

"And no romance between the two of *you*." President Black tousled their hair. "Remember, Glossy and Miss Gee Bee are practically brother and sister."

*****

The maintenance crew set up one of the bargain tables in the middle of the first floor as contest central, cordoning it off with red velvet ropes. Then, the men dumped two full bags of mail on the table, creating a mountain of cards and letters in need of sorting.

It was enough to make the shoppers curious, especially

until Judy from display advertising brought down a sign on a silver pedestal and set it up nearby.

Sweetheart Shopping Spree! Below that, in the big heart in the middle of the sign, it said, *Miss Gee Bee* and *Glossy the Glosser Boy Pick the Winning Poem.* Along the bottom, it said, *Winner Announced on Valentine's Day!*

Just like that, Emily found herself reading love poems in the middle of the Glosser Bros. Department Store with some guy she didn't know.

Named Glossy.

It wasn't exactly how she'd thought her day would go when she'd woken up that morning.

"Here's a good one!" Ryan was reading poems addressed to Miss Gee Bee since there were only a few addressed to Glossy so far. "'Violets are red, roses are blue. In the department store of love, the best bargain is you.'"

Emily groaned and let her head fall forward on the table. "Not again."

"What do you mean, not again?" asked Ryan.

"I mean I've seen *dozens* of versions of that poem in this contest." She rolled her head back and forth, crinkling letters underneath it. "*Hundreds*, even."

"No kidding." Ryan chuckled as he rummaged through the pile. "I wonder if...hey, you're right!" He pulled out a postcard and read it aloud. "'Roses are violets, red is blue. If I couldn't shop at Gee Bee, I don't know what I'd do.'"

Emily raised her head. "I swear, it's like every other

poem is roses and violets. Where's the originality, man?"

Ryan read another one. "'Roses are red, violets are blue. Dear Miss Gee Bee, I love you.'"

An elderly woman was walking by just as he read it and smiled. "That's so sweet, young man. Miss Gee Bee's a lucky woman."

"Thank you, ma'am." Ryan nodded graciously. "And I'm a *very* lucky man."

As the old woman walked away from the table, Ryan and Emily both laughed quietly, into the pile. Another old lady happened by at that exact moment and gave them a cross look, which only made them laugh harder.

When the laughter finally faded, Emily grabbed a postcard and flicked it at him. "So have you done much poetry critiquing before this?"

"Oh my, yes," Ryan answered, putting on a snobbish voice. "I'm a *professional*, actually. I started out critiquing nursery rhymes and moved on from there to commercial jingles."

"You don't say!"

"Oh, but I do," said Ryan. "Sometimes, I even critique people's conversations for the fun of it. You'd never believe how many times the average person says things that are inadequate in one way or another."

"Fascinating." Emily ripped open an envelope and slid out the letter inside. "And how would you rate *my* conversation skills?"

"Pretty good. Especially the part where you called me

a real looker with a dynamite personality and charm that won't quit."

"Hmmm." Emily tapped her chin with a fingertip. "You didn't *tell* me the conversations you critique are in your *imagination.*"

"I didn't think they were." Ryan laughed. "I guess I misheard what you said. Though it's also true I read minds from time to time. You might have been *thinking* those things, though you didn't say them out loud."

"Let's test that interesting theory." Emily narrowed her eyes and leaned toward him. "Can you read what I'm thinking right now?"

"That I'm a really wonderful guy in every possible way?"

Emily shook her head slowly. "Not even close, Glossy."

Just then, Judy returned from the display department, carrying a hatbox. "Hey, guys." She was a few years older than either of them, with blonde hair tied in a ponytail. She wore wire-framed granny glasses like the ones John Lennon had made famous. "I have something for you."

"Ah, you shouldn't have," said Ryan. "Unless it's cash."

"Or candy," said Emily. "I'm starving."

"Even better." Judy opened the box and tipped it toward them. "We just finished these this morning."

It only took a second for Emily to realize what was in the box. "You didn't. Please tell me you didn't."

"I did," said Judy.

"Oh, cool!" Ryan reached into the box and pulled out a black plastic bowler hat. The brim was wide and flat; the crown was printed with a jumble of op art hearts and curlicues. "Just like Miss Gee Bee's hat in the newspaper ads!"

"That's right." Judy reached in and pulled out a second plastic hat—identical except for the brim, which was more of a bill extending from one side. "And for Glossy, we have a *baseball* style hat with the same designs as Miss Gee Bee."

"I love it!" Grinning, Ryan took the hat and stuck it on his head—backwards. "This is perfect for my character!"

Judy turned the hat around so the bill faced forward as it should. "*Now* it's perfect."

Emily put her own hat on and smiled. "How do I look?"

"Very cute," said Judy. "Like Miss Gee Bee come to life."

Ryan reached over and tipped her hat to one side, then did the same for his own. "We match."

He met her gaze then and held it...just for a moment. Just long enough for her to notice something for the first time. A flicker of appreciation? Or was it just her imagination?

And then it was gone.

"So the hats were ordered by President Black." Judy put the lid back on the hat box and pushed it under her right arm. "He wants you to wear them while you're judging the contest or anytime you appear in public as Miss

Gee Bee or Glossy."

"Can do," said Ryan. "But can we take them off when we go to the can?"

Judy laughed. "Up to you, Glossy. Just take care of the darn things. They took forever to work up, and we only have two."

"So no hat frisbee, then?" asked Ryan. "No hat horseshoes?"

"Correct," said Judy.

"But hat tackle football is okay," said Emily.

"Why wouldn't it be?" Judy chuckled.

It was then that a little old lady in a red coat stopped by the velvet rope, beaming. "Oh, heavens! Don't the two of you look wonderful? Just like the Gee Bee lady in the ads!"

"Thank you, ma'am," said Emily.

"Such adorable hats," said the old lady. "I just love all the little hearts on them! Glosser's and Gee Bee really are all about Valentine's Day, aren't they?"

"They sure are, ma'am," said Ryan.

The old lady leaned closer. "And you two make *just* the perfect couple. I wish you *all* the happiness."

Ryan flashed Emily a look. She suddenly realized she was blushing and looked away.

*****

After a few hours of going through love poems on the sales floor, Emily and Ryan went to Glosser's Cafeteria in the Annex for a break. They quickly discovered they had something in common: the soda fountain was their favorite place to eat in the store.

And they both knew the Shaffer twins who worked there, though they couldn't tell them apart.

"Hi, Ruby!" said Ryan as he bounded up to the counter and shook his hat in the air. "What kind of discount do we get if we're wearing these hats?"

"Oh, that's cute," said the twin at the counter. "But I'm Ruth."

"Whoops." Ryan shook the hat again. "So what's the special discount for Glossy the Glosser Boy and Miss Gee Bee?"

Ruth smiled, turned, and called out to her sister, who was just walking out of the kitchen with a tub of ice cream. "What's the special discount for Glossy and Miss Gee Bee?"

Ruby shrugged. "Just the usual employee discount, as far as I know. I could ask the manager, though."

"Or President Black," said Ruth.

"That's okay." Ryan tapped the hat down on his head with an index finger. "The usual employee discount is fine."

"So what would you like?" asked Ruth.

"One hot fudge sundae." Ryan glanced at Emily. "What about you?"

"I'll have the same," said Emily.

"And what else?" asked Ruth and Ruby at the same

time.

"That's all, thanks," said Ryan.

"Okay," said Ruth. "And Ruby, how about throwing in some extra fudge sauce for these two since they missed out on the special discount?"

"You got it." Ruby winked.

It was then Emily realized the Shaffer twins had been teasing them all along.

*****

"Oh my God." Emily put another spoonful of chocolate sauce and vanilla ice cream in her mouth and let it slide down her throat. "I *love* the sundaes here. *And* the banana splits *and* the milkshakes."

"Join the club." Ryan had another scoop of his own sundae and smiled blissfully. "Though I'm a little shocked to hear Miss Gee Bee say that. Aren't you supposed to love the snack bar at Gee Bee more?"

"Glosser's cafeteria is better." Emily leaned toward him and dropped her voice to a whisper. "Don't tell anyone."

"I promise not to tell." Ryan smirked. "Unless I think it will benefit me in some way."

"Just remember, two can play at that game." Emily nodded. "I can always tell on you for liking the restaurant at *Penn Traffic* better."

"But that's a lie!"

"Is it, Ryan? Is it?" Giggling, she spooned more sundae into her mouth, savoring the cold, chocolatey sweetness.

"You're a tough customer, you know that?" said Ryan. "Is that what happens when you grow up on the mean streets of...of..."

"Geistown."

"Ohhh. That *is* mean." It wasn't, not even a little. "That explains a lot about you, Miss Gee Bee."

"Like what?" asked Emily.

"Your hard-bitten attitude." Ryan scowled and shook a fist. "Your intimidating nastiness. Your quick, explosive temper."

"What about the foul language I use every other word?"

"That, too," said Ryan. "Though it *is* hard to be *too* scary when you've got a hot fudge sundae mustache."

Emily laughed, grabbed a napkin, and wiped her mouth. "What about you? What side of the tracks are you from?"

"Kernville," said Ryan. "The mellow part of town."

Kernville, a neighborhood in downtown Johnstown, wasn't mellow at all. "Are you serious?" asked Emily.

"Lived there all my life." Ryan nodded and dug more fudge out of the sundae dish. "Why do you think I'm such a creampuff?"

Emily laughed. She doubted he was any kind of creampuff at all, coming from that tough neighborhood.

"So whereabouts in Kernville do you live?"

"That's confidential information." Ryan narrowed his eyes. "But I *can* tell you it's not far from a great little sub and pizza place."

"Do you mean Brownie's?" Emily grinned. "They're the best in town!"

Ryan shrugged. "Maybe."

"Man of mystery, huh?" She ate a little more fudge from the sundae. "So can you at least tell me about your family? Do you have any brothers or sisters?"

"Let's see." He flicked his spoon as he counted them out loud. "There's Rossy, Bossy, and Mossy. Then my sisters Flossy, Tossy, Hossy, and Lossy. Nice big Catholic family."

"So Glossy is your *real* name." Emily chuckled. "No wonder you were perfect for the job!"

"I'm not surprised you never guessed 'Ryan' is just a nickname. I have *multiple* nicknames, actually: Joe, John, Tom, Ted, Frank, Rob, and Bob...though *most* folks know me as *Rubber Chicken.*"

Emily laughed some more; she did that a lot with Ryan around. There could be *less* fun things than working with him on the contest, she realized.

"I guess we should get back downstairs and keep reading poems." She clinked her spoon in the sundae dish and got up from the table.

"*Or* we could just pick a winner at random and spend the rest of the time goofing around," suggested Ryan.

"And miss out on all the wonderful entries we haven't read yet? Not a chance!"

Ryan shrugged. "Who could stand missing out on all that?"

"Hey, maybe we'll find some great poems yet," said Emily.

"Maybe we will." Ryan smiled. "You never know."

*****

The next day, the judging moved from Glosser Bros. downtown to Gee Bee in Richland. Emily got there bright and early at 8:45, expecting to arrive ahead of Ryan.

But by the time she walked onto the sales floor, he was already there and set up. Wearing his Glossy ball cap, he grinned and waved from behind a product table near the front of the store, just inside the big glass front doors. A sign promoting the contest rose up from the middle of the table, mounted in a silver pedestal frame, with a mountain of mail heaped around it.

"Good morning, Miss Gee Bee!" With a flourish, Ryan dropped an envelope into a white mailsack on the floor. "I hope you don't mind that I took the liberty of getting a head start before you got here."

"How dare you?" she snapped with mock indignation. "What if I missed out on some great poems in the batch you judged on your own?"

"Trust me, you didn't." Ryan opened another

envelope, glanced at the letter inside for a heartbeat, and tossed it in the sack. "You *really* didn't."

Emily joined him at the table and started scanning entries. "You do realize we might have to settle for something that's *the least bad*, right?"

"Have faith, Miss Gee Bee." Ryan deepened his voice, sounding like a hero on TV. "We may yet locate a work of highest quality among all this inferior slush."

"You haven't been doing this as long as I have," said Emily as she dumped the latest letter in the sack. "Believe me, you'll lose that silly optimism soon enough."

"Until then, I choose to look on the bright side." Ryan tipped his hat at a passing customer—a middle-aged woman with brown hair.

The move reminded Emily that she'd left her hat in the car. "Cover for me! I'll be right back!"

She darted out of the store, got the bowler hat from her bright green VW Beetle in the parking lot, and scurried back in, teeth chattering. Running to the car without her coat had been quick, but it was only in the 20s out there.

"I don't believe it," said Ryan when she got back to the sorting table.

Breathless, Emily tugged the plastic bowler hat on her head. "I know! I can't believe I forgot this, either!"

"No, no," said Ryan. "I mean I can't believe *this.*"

In his right hand, he waved a red envelope and a Valentine's Day card with a red heart on the front.

"What?" asked Emily. "Another contest entry?"

"I wouldn't call it *just* another entry." Ryan cleared his throat, opened the card wide, and read what was written inside. "'The stream flows fast from the mountain so vast. The sun shines bright and imbues us with light. The wind blows strong and accomp'nies birds' song. All the world's like a dream, every silver moonbeam, every heart full of love, shines like Heaven above. I just pray you'll soon see, sweet and soft Miss Gee Bee, how you make my soul soar, and embrace me for more.'"

For a moment after he'd finished, neither of them spoke. Then, Emily shook her head slowly, in a daze, and pointed at the card in his hand. "Wow," she said simply. "That's...that's actually..."

"I know." Ryan widened his eyes and nodded. "It's the first good one I've seen so far."

"Yeah, for sure." Emily frowned. "So don't keep me in suspense. Who *wrote* it?"

"Beats the heck outta me." Ryan flapped the envelope in his hand. "No return address. No identification whatsoever. Miss Gee Bee has a *secret admirer*."

"Huh." Emily thought for a moment, then took the envelope from him. "No stamp or postmark, either. Whoever submitted this must have dropped it off at the store."

"It was in the mail bag this morning." Ryan shrugged. "That's all I know."

Emily took the card from him next and scanned the poem. It read as well on paper as it had sounded out loud.

"Do you know what else this means?"

"The contest is over?"

"It means we have to find out *who* this person is," said Emily. "Because he's the only actual poet we've found so far out of hundreds of entries."

"What if he—or she—doesn't *want* to be found?"

"He *does*, trust me," said Emily. "Why else would he send this to Miss Gee Bee?"

"Because he's too shy to come forward?"

"No way." Emily shook the card and envelope in her hand. "He *will*. We haven't heard the last of the *unknown poet*."

*****

The hunt was on. Emily and Ryan combed through the rest of the entries in the mail bag but didn't find another card like the first. They asked around the staff, but none of them remembered seeing anyone dropping off the card that day or the day before. No surprise there; people dropped off entries in a cardboard contest box at the front of the store all the time.

The only clue came when Beth, a salesgirl, recognized the card as one sold in Gee Bee's greeting card department—though narrowing it down from there was next to impossible. Dozens of that same card had been purchased over the Valentine's Day shopping season.

The search was going nowhere fast. Emily and Ryan

decided to talk about it over lunch at the Howard Johnson's restaurant located across the parking lot from Gee Bee.

"It's just so frustrating." Emily grabbed a French fry from her plate and popped it into her mouth. "We finally find someone who can write great poems, and we don't know who it *is*."

"It's enough to drive you crazy, all right." Ryan took a bite of his cheeseburger and chewed thoughtfully.

"What about the security cameras?"

Ryan swallowed and had a sip of cola. "People drop entries in the box all day. Even if we spotted the one who dropped in that particular card, how could we ever actually *identify* him?"

"You're right." Emily sighed and had another fry. "What about fingerprints? Do you have a cop in the family?"

Ryan laughed. "Sorry, my dad and brother both work at the mill."

"Really?" Emily brightened. "Which one?"

"Bethlehem," said Ryan. "The car shop."

"My dad works at Bethlehem, too! He's in the bar, rod, and wire mill." He was also a boss, though she didn't mention that part.

"Just about everybody works in the mills around here," said Ryan. "Bethlehem, U.S. Steel, whatever."

Emily tipped her head to one side as she watched him. "What about you? Are you waiting to get in?"

Ryan shook his head. "Get *out*, is more like it. I don't

want anything to do with working at the mill. I want to move away and live a *different* life."

"Doing what?" asked Emily.

Ryan shrugged. "What about you? What do *you* want to do?"

"I don't know." Emily picked up another fry and twirled it between her thumb and forefinger. "I went to college for a while...UPJ. But then I sort of stopped going. It just wasn't doing it for me, y'know?"

"Have you thought about moving away?"

Emily nodded. "I just can't seem to make up my mind, though. At least being Miss Gee Bee's kind of fun."

"Maybe you should consider being a detective," said Ryan. "If you can solve the mystery of the unknown poet, at least."

Emily sighed. "I keep feeling like I'm *missing* something. Like if I could just put my finger on it, I could crack the case."

"I know exactly what you mean." Ryan raised his soda cup in a toast. "Maybe the two of us working together will get to the truth."

Emily smiled and raised her cup, too. "Here, here." Then, the two of them tapped their cups together, completing the toast.

*****

The next day, Sunday, Glosser's and Gee Bee were

closed—but Emily and Ryan couldn't wait to continue their investigation. They met at Glosser Bros. downtown and talked the security guard into letting them in so they could check the latest deposits in the contest box.

Sure enough, they found a red envelope near the top of the box, addressed with familiar handwriting, with no return address or other form of identification. The card inside wasn't identical to the previous one; it featured a cupid with bow and arrow instead of a big red heart.

But the poem written inside certainly had a familiar style and quality. Reading it aloud, Emily had no doubt in her mind that it was from the same person who'd written the first.

"'Tell me there's no tomorrow, and I might cry. Say I'm due for prison, and I might lie. Give me cause for battle, and I might try. But tell me there's no Miss Gee Bee, and I will die.'"

"Nice," said Lou the security guard. "Very romantic."

"There's more," said Emily. "'If the world in all its turning stops, and every flower wilts...if the stars turn all the seas to steam, and every mountain tilts...if every dream of every joy turns nightmare through and through...I still with every breath and pulse turn every thought to you.'"

"Can I borrow that for my wife?" asked Lou.

"That's him, all right," said Emily. "That's our man."

"Hey, Lou," said Ryan. "You didn't happen to see whoever put that card in the box, did you?"

Lou, a scrawny old man with gray hair and blotchy,

reddish complexion, shook his head. "Nobody's in the store overnight during my shift. Whoever puts in those cards and letters—I don't ever see them."

"Damn," said Ryan. "I wish there was some way to monitor the entries as they come in."

"I can't think of any," said Lou. "It's a busy store during the day."

"Plus, he doesn't always drop them off here," said Emily. "He takes them to Gee Bee, too."

Ryan rummaged through the other mail on the contest table. "Let's see if he left us any others while we're here."

"Then I'm gonna have to show you out," said Lou. "The Glossers come in to work on Sunday sometimes, you know."

*****

"What do we do next?" asked Emily as Lou locked the doors behind them.

"Go for a walk in the park?" Ryan bowed and gestured at Johnstown's little Central Park across the street.

Emily shrugged, smiled, and went with him.

It was a cold day with gray, cloudy skies, but at least no snow was falling. As the two of them entered the park, the frosty puffs of their breath in the air were their only company.

"Do you think we'll ever find the unknown poet?" asked Emily.

"I honestly don't know," said Ryan.

"But we *have* to. We can't give up!"

"I knew you'd say that." Ryan smiled.

"Really?" Emily laughed. "But we've only known each other a few days."

"Sometimes that's all it takes." Ryan met her gaze. "Sometimes, you just *know* somebody from the start."

Emily looked away. What was it about him that made her blush sometimes?

"You think we should just give up trying to find him?" she asked. "Do you think it's a waste of time?"

"Not at all." His voice changed a little, grew steadier and warmer. "As long as I'm spending time with you, it's never a waste."

Startled, Emily looked back over at him. Was he saying what she *thought* he was? Until now, she'd only considered the possibility in the abstract, in the back of her mind.

"Thanks," she said simply.

"It's been fun, hasn't it?" said Ryan. "Working together, solving the mystery. We, uh...we make a good team, don't we?"

She only had to think for a second. "Sure." She couldn't deny it. "We do."

"Just like when two people are solving a crime in a movie," said Ryan. "They investigate and find clues, and the mystery deepens." He stopped in front of the gazebo and turned to face her. "Then they have a moment where he takes her hand." He reached for her hand, and she didn't pull it away. "Then the music swells, and he tells her how he really feels."

Emily's heart pounded. She was caught up in the magic of the moment, the feel of his hand, the sparkle in his eyes...the wondering what would come next.

Ryan leaned closer. The mist of his breath mingled with hers as he spoke.

"Then he tells her he's come to care for her, and he can't stop thinking about her, and he can't bear to be without her." He smiled.

Emily thought he might kiss her. If he'd tried, would she have pulled away?

She didn't get to find out.

Ryan was the one to pull away and let go of her hand. "Do you know the movies I'm talking about?" he asked.

Emily nodded.

"I love those movies," said Ryan, and then he kept walking.

Her legs were only a little bit shaky as she caught up to him and walked along the winding path by his side.

*****

It was starting to look like the unknown poet would not be revealed in time to win the contest.

Another of his poems arrived Monday, as good as the first two, but again no clues to his identity could be found. None of the other entries came close to that quality, either;

no one else was worthy of being declared the winner.

By Tuesday morning, the day before Valentine's Day, Emily was on the verge of losing hope. It was the last day entries would be accepted. If she didn't unmask the poet then, it seemed to her the odds of *ever* unmasking him would be much lower.

Either way, the contest would soon be over. So would her work with Ryan—at least until another promotion came around that required them to reunite. Thinking about that upset her almost as much as thinking about never solving the unknown poet mystery.

With so much on her mind, she hadn't slept well the night before, and she'd gotten up much too early. Rather than sit around and stew, she decided to drive to Gee Bee early and get started with her day.

The store didn't open until ten that day, but Emily was able to get in through the employee entrance around the back of the place. Hurrying through the store, she smiled at the thought of beating Ryan to work for a change. At least *that* little victory would give her a boost.

But even arriving an hour early wasn't enough, it turned out. Emily charged out of the employee locker room and headed for the front of the store, ready for an early start though Gee Bee wasn't open for the day yet.

Just as she rushed past a cluster of clothing racks, however, she caught sight of Ryan already stationed at the contest table, bent over his work.

Emily shook her head, wondering how early she had to

be to beat him. At least she had the element of surprise in her favor, though, if revenge was on her mind.

Which it was.

Slowly, she sneaked through the women's clothing racks behind him, holding her breath. She came up close, crouched and ready to spring with a shout.

It was then that she saw what he was doing, and she froze. Her eyes shot wide open, and her heart raced even faster.

As Emily watched, he wrote something in a Valentine's card, then slipped it into a red envelope, licked the flap, and sealed it. Then, he placed the envelope with the card inside on top of the pile of mail on the table in front of him.

Emily was so stunned, she dropped the Miss Gee Bee hat she'd been carrying. Ryan heard it hit the floor and looked her way instantly.

"Good morning!" He grinned and waved as if she hadn't caught him red-handed. As if she hadn't fully understood what he'd just been up to. "You're here early! What's the occasion?"

Frowning, Emily picked up her hat but didn't put it on. Then, she walked up to the table and stared at the red envelope on top of the pile.

Ryan saw what she was looking at and grabbed it. "Oh, hey! Looks like we got another card from that poet, huh?"

Emily nodded.

"Why don't you go ahead and read it?" Ryan offered

her the card. "The contest ends today, so this should be the last one we get."

She accepted the envelope from him and slit open the flap with a fingernail. The card, when she pulled it out, bore the image of a heart-shaped box of candy and a single red rose on a candlelit table, as if in preparation for a romantic dinner.

Opening the card, she saw another poem inside.

"Go ahead and read it out loud," said Ryan.

"I know it was you," said Emily. "I saw you writing the card."

"Just read it," said Ryan. "Please."

She took another look at the card, and her eyes were drawn to the few lines at the bottom, after the poem. "You signed it. Your put your name and address on it."

"Right. It's time to come clean."

"Why bother?" Emily glared at him. "You're a *judge*. You can't *win* the *contest*."

"That's not why I did it. Why I did *any* of it. I don't *want* the shopping spree."

"Then why *did* you do it?"

"Because of how I feel about *you*," said Ryan. "You *inspire* me. I *care* about you, Emily."

"You show you care for someone by *lying* to them? *Pretending* you don't know who's writing the poems?"

He looked rattled as he tried to explain. "But the *poems* don't lie. I mean, at first, I was hoping to get the bonus, but then I *fell* for you. My poems are all about how I truly *feel* about you, and..."

"What bonus?" Emily felt herself inching toward a terrible storm, a hurricane the likes of which she'd never known before.

"The *bonus*," Ryan said matter-of-factly. "*You* know. For having the winning poem written in your honor."

Emily still couldn't believe what she was hearing. "There's a *bonus?*"

"I was originally going to write poems to *myself*," explained Ryan. "I figured that even if the winning writer remained anonymous and didn't get the shopping spree, I could still at least get the bonus for being the subject of the winning poem. But when I met *you*, I wanted *you* to have the bonus. And I wanted you to know how I *felt* about you."

"No one *told* me about a *bonus*," snapped Emily.

"But the bonus doesn't matter," said Ryan. "All that matters are the *poems* and how I *feel* about..."

"Maybe the bonus would have *mattered* if I'd known it *existed*." Emily was furious. All her good feelings about the poems, about Ryan, were out the window. She was so upset, nothing made sense to her anymore; everything seemed like a blur of betrayal, lies, and secrets.

"Look, I didn't know you didn't know about that," said Ryan. "I *swear*."

"Oh my God." She backed away from him. "How could I have been so *wrong* about you? About *everything?*"

"Emily, please..."

"I can't *look* at you right now. I can't *stand* you." She turned and ran off through the store. "I need to get *away* from you!"

With that, she left him standing by the contest table with its mountain of cards and letters, watching her go with the saddest look on his face. Atop his head, he wore his plastic Glossy ball cap, its happy pattern of stylized hearts and curlicues the opposite of the true feelings swirling in his head at that moment.

*****

Emily found herself wandering through the produce department of the Gee Bee supermarket, which was located next-door to the department store. By then, the anger had let up a little, at least enough that she could finally think clearly again. But that didn't mean she was any happier about the situation.

She still couldn't believe what Ryan had told her—not only that he'd never mentioned the bonus, but that he'd been trying to get it for himself.

Why had no one mentioned the bonus to her until now? For that matter, how could he have just stood there, day after day, and gone through those poems with her, never mentioning that he was the unknown poet? It bothered her on every level, especially because she'd started to think fondly of him.

She thought of the day when they'd gone walking in

Central Park and he'd taken her hand and looked into her eyes. There had been a feeling there, something she hadn't wanted to turn away from. Even before then, she'd noticed he was different from other guys and that there might be some kind of connection between them. It was one of the reasons she'd enjoyed going through the contest entries and trying to pick a winner, even though it was kind of a tedious task.

Now here she was, having been lied to, having been fooled by someone whom she thought she might have been developing positive feelings for.

Here she was in the produce department, watching the housewives pick out potatoes, onions, lettuce, and other vegetables, while her heart raced from the stress of the day.

What was she going to do next? Give up on her job at Gee Bee? To what end? To prove a point, that a woman had as much right as a man to know about bonuses and to be paid equal to a man for the same work? Or should she just move on and look for a better situation elsewhere? Should she look for a better workplace where she might be better appreciated, and even another co-worker who might be a better friend to her...or more?

Even as she was embroiled in these troubling thoughts, a friendly voice popped up behind her. "Hey Emily!" Tina Fontana stepped in front of her, smiled, and waved. "What's up? How's the contest going, Miss Gee Bee?"

"Not so great," said Emily. "To be honest, it's pretty awful right now."

"What do you mean?" asked Tina. "It looked like you and Ryan were having a good time out there, going through those cards and letters."

"It wasn't as much fun as I thought," said Emily. "*He* wasn't as much fun as I thought at first, either."

"Why?" asked Tina. "What happened?"

"It's a long story," said Emily. "Basically, there was bonus money involved, and nobody bothered to tell me about it. Ryan wasn't being up front with me about a *lot* of things."

"Like what?" asked Tina.

"*He* was writing some of the poems," said Emily, "and he let me think it was someone else. We were both working to try to figure out who the mystery poet was, and the whole time, it was him!"

"You gotta be kidding me." Tina's long blonde hair swayed as she shook her head in disgust. "Well, at least you won't have to worry about *him* anymore, the jerk!"

Emily frowned. "Why do you say that?"

"He just *quit*," said Tina. "No explanation, either, according to Mr. Shepherd...at least until now."

The information caught Emily off guard. Her first instinct was to say *Good riddance*...but then she didn't. Something made her hold back.

"Aren't you gonna thank me for the good news?" asked Tina. "At least you won't have to deal with that idiot anymore."

"Yeah, thanks." Suddenly, unexpectedly, Emily felt

adrift. The rage that had boiled over in her earlier was just gone.

"Why aren't you happier about this, hon? Miss Gee Bee is victorious! Glossy the Glosser Boy is history! That's a *good* thing, right?"

Why did Emily hesitate? "I don't know." Why wasn't she jumping for joy?

"Aw, you're just a little wired." Tina put an arm around her shoulders and gave her a squeeze. "It'll be okay, don't worry. Let's celebrate tonight at Freddie's or Mynderbinders, and you'll feel better."

Just then, a deep voice spoke up behind them, one they knew all too well. "Celebrate what?"

Turning, they saw the store manager, Jack Shepherd, staring back at them. The middle-aged man with thinning brown hair, a thick brown mustache, and a pot belly under his short-sleeved white button-down shirt did not look amused.

"Nothing in particular," Tina said flippantly.

Mr. Shepherd folded his arms over his chest. "It wouldn't have anything to do with Ryan leaving Glosser Bros., would it?"

"Absolutely not," said Tina.

Emily shook her head.

"Did something happen between you two?" asked Mr. Shepherd.

Again, Emily shook her head.

Mr. Shepherd scowled as if he knew she was holding

back, but he didn't press it. "So who won the contest? Ryan said you picked the winner."

"He did?" Emily was confused.

"Yep. He also said the winning poem was written for Miss Gee Bee, so you get the bonus."

"What bonus?" asked Emily.

"Didn't I tell you?" Mr. Shepherd unfolded his arms and stuck his hands in his pants pockets. "I guess I must've forgotten." He looked a little sheepish.

"Huh." Tina gave Emily a meaningful glance. "Imagine that."

"Anyway, it's just fifty bucks," said Mr. Shepherd. "Ryan wanted to make sure you got it."

Emily stood there for a long moment, processing what she's heard. The rage that had been roaring through her was transforming, becoming another emotion altogether.

Apparently, things weren't as cut and dried as she'd at first thought. Maybe it was time for her to write a new draft of her reaction to the situation.

"Mr. Shepherd?" she said. "May I have the rest of the day off, please?"

"Sure, why not?" Mr. Shepherd pursed his lips and stuck his hands on his hips. "You're not exactly getting any work done right now anyway, are you?"

"I have one more favor to ask," said Emily. "Could you give me Ryan's home address? He forgot something when he left."

*****

Emily had to double-check the address on Franklin Street in Kernville when she got there.

Then, she laughed out loud.

As she got out of her car and headed for the front door, she shook her head. Leave it to Ryan, with his crazy sense of humor, to give *this* as his home address.

But sure enough, he was there when she walked in the place, sitting at a table across the room. He was reading a thick book with a tattered green cover and the title "Shakespearean Sonnets" in faded gold leaf on the spine.

When he looked up, she could tell he was surprised to see her. Worried, too. "Emily?"

"You *said* you lived near a great sub and pizza place," she told him. "But I never would've *guessed* you lived *in* Brownie's Bar!"

The surprise faded from his eyes, though the worry lingered. "Be it ever so humble." He shrugged.

"Not so humble at all, if you ask me. My stomach is growling just standing here!"

"I have found no sweeter perfume in all of Johnstown." He closed his eyes and inhaled deeply. "Hot Italian sub number five."

Emily felt a little awkward standing there and sat down across from him. "So where do you *really* live?"

"Across the street, I think." He frowned. "Or is that up the block and over the bridge? I can't keep track."

"Well, I'm glad I found you." Emily took a deep breath to calm her nerves. "There's something I wanted to talk to you about."

Ryan looked like he thought about leaving, but he didn't. "If it's about the contest, I..."

Emily held up a hand. "Just listen."

He opened his mouth to say something, then closed it.

"I just wanted to say...I know you're not the reason I didn't know about the bonus. Mr. Shepherd forgot to mention it, and I guess President Black must've assumed I already knew."

Ryan shifted restlessly on his chair. "Okay."

Emily took another deep breath and let it out slowly. "I also wanted to thank you for the poems. I mean, you could've just told me they were yours to begin with..."

"I know," said Ryan. "I'm sorry."

"...but they were still very sweet." She met his gaze. "Very romantic."

Again, he looked surprised. "You still like them?"

"Good question." Emily reached into the pocket of her coat and pulled out a red envelope. "Maybe this will shed some light on the matter." She slid the envelope across the table to him.

Frowning, he opened it and took out the card inside. This one had two swans on the front, beaks touching, their heads and necks forming the shape of a heart.

As he read it silently, eyes scanning each line she had written. Emily didn't need to hear it aloud to remember each heartfelt word:

Roses are red,
Violets are blue,
Gee Bee goes with Glosser's
Like I go with you.

It was enough to make Ryan laugh out loud. Emily laughed along with him, then reached over and covered his hand with her own.

"Glossy, will you split a Brownie's pizza with me?" she asked.

"Only if we can get a Shaffer twins sundae at Glosser's Cafeteria for dessert, Miss Gee Bee," said Ryan.

Then he leaned toward her, impulsively going in for a kiss.

Impulsively, she kissed him back.

Gee Bee Photo Gallery

Photos courtesy William Glosser

VALENTINE'S DAY AT GLOSSER'S

ABOUT THE AUTHOR

Author and editor Robert Jeschonek grew up in Johnstown, Pennsylvania and spent many happy hours as a kid in the Glosser Bros. Department Store. Since then, he has gone on to write lots of books and stories, including *Long Live Glosser's, Penn Traffic Forever, Christmas at Glosser's, Easter at Glosser's, Halloweeen at Glosser's, A Glosser's Christmas Love Story, Fear of Rain, Richland Mall Rules,* and *Death By Polka* (which are all set in and around Johnstown). He has written a lot of other cool stuff, too, including *Star Trek* and *Doctor Who* fiction and *Batman* comics. His young adult fantasy novel, *My Favorite Band Does Not Exist,* won a Forward National Literature Award and was named a top ten first novel for youth by *Booklist* magazine. His work has been published around the world in over a hundred books, e-books, and audio books. You can find out more about them at his website, www.robertjeschonek.com, or by looking up his name on Facebook, Twitter, or Google. As you'll see, he's kind of crazy...in a *good* way.

ANOTHER GREAT JOHNSTOWN
STORY NOW AVAILABLE FROM
ROBERT JESCHONEK

A GLOSSER'S CHRISTMAS LOVE STORY

BY ROBERT JESCHONEK

With her fiancé far away fighting a war in Korea, Sarah faces a blue Christmas in Johnstown, Pennsylvania in 1953. But going to work as an elf at Glosser's Department Store turns her holiday upside-down. Santa Claus, played by fellow employee Frank, falls beard over sleighbells for her. When the magic of the season at Glosser's lights a spark of romance between them, Sarah is torn between the man at war and the one in the St. Nick outfit. On the night before Christmas, she must make a fateful choice that changes everything...and leads her to a crossroads 63 years later at the famous musical Christmas tree in Johnstown's Central Park.

AND NOW, A SPECIAL PREVIEW OF A GLOSSER'S CHRISTMAS LOVE STORY...

Johnstown, 1953

"You dropped something." The young man with the bright green eyes and red hair held up a 20-lb. frozen turkey and grinned. "Here you go."

Sarah Jensen stopped in the frozen food aisle of the Glosser Bros. grocery store and shook her head. "Not *my* turkey, thanks."

"But it is!" The guy pushed the frozen turkey toward her. "I clearly saw it fall out of the pocket of your sweater."

Sarah shrugged and sighed. She wasn't in the mood to goof around that morning, not after the letter she'd gotten before coming to work. "You must be confusing me with someone else."

"Not a chance." The guy's smile turned charming. "There's *no way* I could ever confuse you with anyone else."

The smile made Sarah hesitate. She was 23 years old, after all, and he was...he was...

Not completely unattractive. His eyes were bright as emeralds, his hair red as firelight. He was six feet tall, with a slim, athletic build and muscular shoulders. And he was about her age or a little younger, perhaps a little older.

But no. She had her reasons for not socializing these days. And besides... "I need to get back to my register," she told him. "My lunch break is over."

"So?" He lowered the turkey, revealing the Glosser Bros. nametag pinned to the chest of his white button-down shirt. "I'm not even *on* break."

The tag, stamped with the name "Frank," caught Sarah off guard. She hadn't known he was a fellow employee. She'd never even seen him before he shoved the turkey in her face.

Not that it made any difference. "Look, I really have to get back to my register," she said.

"Then what am I supposed to do with *this?*" He turned the turkey over in his hands, looking forlorn.

It was then she was seized by the inexplicable impulse to throw him a bone. "Put it in the oven for six and a half hours at 325," she said. "Either that, or roll it down the aisle and use it to bowl for customers."

"Brilliant!" Frank perked up. "You're a genius..." He peered at the nametag pinned to Sarah's gray sweater. "... you *Sarah*, you."

"That's what they tell me." Sarah smirked. "I'm a genius, all right."

As she started to walk away, Frank stepped in front of

her. "See you around?" He smiled expectantly.

"I guess so." Reaching up, she pushed a lock of her chestnut brown hair behind her right ear. "Though I've never seen you around before today."

"That's because this is my first day on the job." He winked. "But you'll be seeing me a lot more from now on."

"Is that so?" Sarah looked toward the checkouts in the front of the store. If she didn't get back to her post soon, someone would come looking for her.

"Absolutely." Frank nodded enthusiastically. "I'm like a bad penny. I keep turning up."

Sarah shrugged and headed for the checkouts. Frank backed away and disappeared in the frozen food department.

Up front, she returned to her register, apologizing for being late to the girl who'd been covering for her. The girl, a chatty redhead, didn't seem to care as she stepped away from the checkout and Sarah replaced her.

As the next customer put her items on the counter, Sarah punched their prices into the register. She slid cans of corn and green beans into the bagging area at the end of the counter, and someone caught them.

At first, Sarah didn't look to see who was doing the bagging. But as she finished ringing everything up, she turned...and there he was.

Frank Halloran himself grinned back at her as he loaded the items into big brown paper bags.

Sarah just stared. She hadn't expected to see him there.

"Ma'am?" Frank was talking to the customer. "Shall I carry these upstairs for you?" Offering to haul purchases was expected, since the grocery store was located in the basement of Glosser's department store. It was a long walk up and out to the parking lot or on-street parking, especially with a heavy load of groceries.

"Yes, please." The customer, a heavyset middle-aged woman in a pale green coat and squat cream hat, nodded. "My car is out back in the lot." With that, she paid Sarah, got her receipt, and briskly started toward the nearby flight of stairs to the first floor.

Frank followed with a bag in each arm. He winked at Sarah as he followed the customer, mouthing four words that made her smile in spite of herself.

Penny for your thoughts?

*****

What happens next? Find out in A GLOSSER'S CHRISTMAS LOVE STORY, on sale now!

If you liked this book, you'll *love* these!

LONG LIVE GLOSSER'S

CHRISTMAS AT GLOSSER'S

EASTER AT GLOSSER'S

HALLOWEEN AT GLOSSER'S

PENN TRAFFIC FOREVER
(A History of the Penn Traffic Department Store)

RICHLAND MALL RULES
(A History of the Richland Mall in Johnstown)

THE GLORY OF GABLE'S
(A History of Altoona's Gable's Department Store)

FEAR OF RAIN
(A Johnstown Flood Story)

THE MASKED FAMILY
(A Cambria County Story)

NOW ON SALE EVERYWHERE ONLINE
OR BY REQUEST AT YOUR LOCAL BOOKSTORE
Ask your bookseller to search by title at Amazon,
Ingram, or Baker and Taylor.

pie press publishing

www.ingramcontent.com/pod-product-compliance
Lightning Source LLC
Chambersburg PA
CBHW022053170626
46808CB00003B/1455